Little Bear's Valentine

Maurice Sendak's Little Bear: *Little Bear's Valentine*
Copyright © 2003 by Nelvana
Based on the animated television series *Little Bear* produced by Nelvana.
™Wild Things Productions
Little Bear characters © 2003 by Maurice Sendak
Based on the series of books written by Else Holmelund Minarik and illustrated by Maurice Sendak
Licensed by Nelvana Marketing Inc.
All rights reserved. Printed in the U.S.A.
www.harperchildrens.com

Library of Congress Cataloging-in-Publication Data
Minarik, Else Holmelund.
   Little Bear's valentine / written by Else Holmelund Minarik ; pictures by Heather Green.
      p.   cm. (Maurice Sendak's Little Bear)
  "HarperFestival."
  "Based on the animated television series Little Bear produced by Nelvana."
  "Based on the series of books written by Else Holmelund Minarik and illustrated by Maurice Sendak."
  Summary: Little Bear looks forward to giving his mother a valentine and to figuring out who the secret admirer is who sent him one.
  ISBN 0-694-01712-4 — ISBN 0-06-052244-5 (lib. bdg.)
  [1. Valentine's Day—Fiction. 2. Mothers and sons—Fiction. 3. Bears—Fiction. 4. Animals—Fiction.]
I. Green, Heather, ill. II. Title. III. Series.
PZ7.M652 Lje 2003 [E]—dc21 2002011577

1 2 3 4 5 6 7 8 9 10
❖
First Edition

Little Bear's Valentine

BY ELSE HOLMELUND MINARIK
ILLUSTRATED BY HEATHER GREEN

HarperCollins*Publishers*

On a cold and snowy Valentine's Day, it's best to be inside where it's warm. That's where Little Bear was. He was sitting at the table, making valentines for all his friends.

The cozy room smelled so good because Mother Bear was baking cookies.

Little Bear made valentines—for Emily, for Hen, for Owl, and for Duck. Little Bear cut his valentines very carefully. And on each card, he drew a little bear. They were all beautiful!

But for Mother Bear, he made the most beautiful valentine of all:
a pink valentine with flowers.

Soon, Little Bear was ready to deliver the valentines he had made for his friends. He decided to surprise Mother Bear with her valentine when he came back home. Where could he hide it? In the cookie jar—of course.

Mother Bear said, "Come here, Little Bear. Let me bundle you up before you go." As he left, she said, "Why don't you look in the mailbox first. There might be a valentine for you there."

"A valentine for me?" Little Bear asked. He wasn't sure which was more fun—to give valentines or to get them.

"Oh, look, Mother Bear! A valentine for me! A beautiful valentine!" Little Bear opened the card—but there was no name in it. Who could have sent it?

Mother Bear said, "You have a secret admirer!"

Little Bear walked along. It was so cold he could see his own breath, but the sun warmed his little face. He was happy, because he had a secret admirer. Who could it be?

It must be someone who likes to keep secrets—but nice ones.

Little Bear thought that being someone's secret admirer is a very nice secret to keep.

Little Bear decided to deliver Emily's valentine first. He liked
Emily. She liked him. Could she be his secret admirer?

    "Oh!" said Emily. "How sweet of you, Little Bear. Here is yours."
She gave him a valentine.

    "Thank you, Emily," said Little Bear. "But I thought maybe you
were my secret admirer!"

Little Bear told Emily all about his special valentine.

"Oh, my goodness," said Emily. "Aren't you lucky! I love secrets!"

"Well," said Little Bear, "I guess I do, too! Good-bye, Emily. I'm off to give Hen her valentine."

"Hello, Little Bear," said Hen, as Little Bear came up the walk.
Little Bear thought, *I wonder if Hen is my secret admirer?*

Little Bear smiled at Hen and said, "Dear Hen, here's your Valentine's Day card." Hen was so pleased.

Hen had something for Little Bear, too. It was a valentine cookie. "I made that for you, Little Bear," said Hen.

So Little Bear told Hen about his secret admirer.

Little Bear had more valentines to deliver.
He had one for Duck and one for Owl.

And so he went on his way.

At the pond, Little Bear gave Duck her valentine.
"Oh, goody!" said Duck. "I love valentines!"
Little Bear held his breath and waited.

But Duck wasn't Little Bear's secret admirer. She had made
a special valentine for him with her own webbed feet.

There was only one card left—for Owl. By now, Little Bear
was very, very curious about his secret admirer. But Owl
couldn't even wait for Little Bear to say, "Hello." He handed
Little Bear a card right away and said, "Happy Valentine's Day,
Little Bear."

Little Bear gave Owl his card. Then, he told Owl all about his secret admirer.

"How exciting," said Owl. "It's a mystery."

"I'm confused!" said Little Bear. He thought about the valentines that Emily, Hen, Duck, and Owl had given to him. They were lovely, but who was his secret admirer?

It was growing late, and Little Bear was getting hungry. He remembered Mother Bear's cookies, so he started for home.

When he walked into the kitchen, all his friends and his very own Mother Bear were there.

Mother Bear said, "Surprise, Little Bear! I am your secret admirer!"

Little Bear got his valentine out of the cookie jar and ran to
Mother Bear. He jumped into her arms and gave her the valentine.
He also gave her a kiss.

"That's from your not-so-secret admirer—me!" he told her. And
she gave him a big kiss back.